Turkey Trouble

"Does this mean we have to eat Tom for Thanksgiving?" Elizabeth asked.

Dad nodded. "I can't insult Mr. Kiebel by refusing his gift. That turkey is so big, he must be worth a lot of money. It was a generous present, and we're going to accept it."

Elizabeth looked very sad. So did Mom.

"Let's go say hello to Tom," Elizabeth suggested quietly.

"OK," I agreed.

When Elizabeth and I stepped outside, Tom ran right up to us. I rested my head against his feathery side.

"Don't worry, Tom," I whispered to him. "We're not going to give up. We'll think of another way to save you."

I didn't tell Tom that time was running out. Thanksgiving was only three days away.

Bantam Books in the SWEET VALLEY KIDS series

SWEET VALLEY KIDS
SUPER SPECIAL

SAVE THE TURKEY!

Written by
Molly Mia Stewart

Created by
FRANCINE PASCAL

Illustrated by
Ying-Hwa Hu

BANTAM BOOKS
NEW YORK·TORONTO·LONDON·SYDNEY·AUCKLAND

RL 2, 005-008

SAVE THE TURKEY!

A Bantam Book / November 1995

*Sweet Valley High® and Sweet Valley Kids® are
registered trademarks of Francine Pascal*

Conceived by Francine Pascal

*Produced by Daniel Weiss Associates, Inc.
33 West 17th Street
New York, NY 10011*

Cover art by Susan Tang

ISBN: 0-553-48286-6

Published simultaneously in the United States and Canada

Bantam Books are published by Bantam Books, a division of Bantam
Doubleday Dell Publishing Group, Inc. Its trademark, consisting of the
words "Bantam Books" and the portrayal of a rooster, is registered in the
U.S. Patent and Trademark Office and in other countries. Marca
Registrada. Bantam Books, 1540 Broadway, New York, New York 10036.

PRINTED IN THE UNITED STATES OF AMERICA

OPM   0 9 8 7 6 5 4 3 2 1

To Jean Yves Santini

CHAPTER 1

Wanted: One Turkey

"Tomorrow is Thursday," I said at the dinner table. "That means Thanksgiving is only one week away. I can't wait!"

Elizabeth smiled. "It's going to be great."

Hi! It's me. Jessica Wakefield.

Elizabeth is my twin sister. We are *identical* twins. That means Elizabeth looks just like me, and I look just like Elizabeth! We both have blue-green eyes and long blond hair with bangs.

We were also born on the same day. We are seven years old.

I love clothes. Elizabeth and I have a bunch that match. When we dress the same way, nobody can tell us apart. Sometimes we can even fool Mom and Dad and our big brother, Steven.

Elizabeth and I are in second grade at Sweet Valley Elementary School. Our teacher is Mrs. Otis. I sit right next to Elizabeth in class.

I like school for two reasons: recess and lunch. Those are the times I can play with my friends. Elizabeth likes *everything* about school—even the boring parts. Even homework! Elizabeth always does hers without being told. I hardly ever do.

My favorite friends at school are Lila Fowler and Ellen Riteman. They like to play with dolls and wear pretty clothes, just like I do.

Elizabeth's favorite school friends are Amy Sutton and Todd Wilkins. Amy and Elizabeth ride horses together. I don't like horses. They smell. Todd and Elizabeth are on the same soccer team. Elizabeth never misses a game. Not even when the field is muddy. Yuck!

Elizabeth acts like a tomboy sometimes. Not me! On the playground, I like to jump rope, play hopscotch, or swing on the swings. I also like to play the piano. I'm going to be an actress or a singer when I grow up. I'll have millions of adoring fans. Maybe I'll be a princess.

A lot of people are surprised that Elizabeth and I are so different. They think we should be the same on the *inside* because we look the same on the *outside*. That's silly. No one else in the world is just like me.

Elizabeth and I are best friends. We're going to be best friends forever. I love being a twin, and so does she.

Do you know what else we love? Thanksgiving! I get to wear my prettiest clothes for the most important dinner of the year. Elizabeth sets the table with our fanciest dishes. And we both love all the delicious things to eat!

"When are we going to go grocery shopping for Thanksgiving dinner?" I asked Mom and Dad.

Dad took a sip of iced tea. Then he said, "Probably this weekend."

"Goody!" I said. "Can I pick out the turkey? I want a really big one so we'll have lots of leftovers."

"Sorry," Mom said. "You can't pick out a turkey."

"Why not?" I demanded.

"Because we're not having turkey," Dad said.

I couldn't believe it. "What do you mean?"

"I'm going to make my famous zucchini lasagna for Thanksgiving this year," Dad announced. "We haven't had it in a long time."

"But it's Thanksgiving," I wailed. "We have to eat turkey."

I looked at Elizabeth. She *had* to be as upset as I was. She was carefully biting into a cherry tomato. She looked perfectly happy.

"Don't *you* think we should have turkey?" I asked, turning to Steven.

Food is very important to my brother. He eats like an entire drove of pigs. I was one thousand percent positive he would agree with me.

But Steven just shrugged. "There's no law that says you have to eat turkey on Thanksgiving," he said. "Besides, Dad's lasagna is really good."

"Mom!" I yelled.

"Honey, why are you getting so upset?" Mom asked. "You love lasagna."

"Not on Thanksgiving, I don't," I said firmly. "On Thanksgiving I only like turkey."

"A little change will be good for you," Mom said.

What was *that* supposed to mean?

Sometimes I do not understand my family. Didn't they know it wouldn't be Thanksgiving without turkey? Well, I did! And I was going to make sure we had one.

CHAPTER 2

A Great Gift

"Come play with us!" I yelled to Dad after school the next afternoon. Elizabeth and I were playing in the pool. Mom was reading a book on the deck. Steven was at his friend Bob's house.

Dad had just come home from work. He had gone inside to change out of his work clothes and come out wearing his bathing suit. Elizabeth and I were surprised. Dad usually only swims on weekends.

"The water's warm!" Elizabeth called.

Without even testing the water, Dad

jumped in. "Brr, it's freezing!" he cried when he came up.

I giggled.

"Fooled you!" Elizabeth said.

"I'll get you for that!" Dad splashed us. Elizabeth and I splashed back. It turned into a gigantic splash battle. Dad won.

Next, Dad gave us piggyback rides. Then he threw us up in the air so we could fly.

I love playing with Dad in the pool. But by then we were getting cold. We all got out of the water. Elizabeth and I lay on the deck in the sun. That's a very good way to warm up.

Dad sat in the chair next to Mom.

"How was work today?" Mom asked him.

"Terrific!" Dad answered. "Something exciting happened."

"What?" Elizabeth asked.

"Well, I have a client named Mr. Kiebel," Dad said. (Clients are the people who come to Dad for help. Dad is a lawyer. That means he knows lots of stuff about the law.)

"I think you told me about him," Mom said. "He's a farmer, right?"

"Right," Dad said. "He grows tomatoes. Unfortunately, his fields are very close to a river. Remember those big rainstorms we had recently?"

Mom and Elizabeth nodded. So did I. About a month earlier, it had rained for a whole week. It was the worst! We couldn't go outside for recess all that time. Water had got into our basement, too.

"Mr. Kiebel's fields were flooded during the storms," Dad said. "All of his tomato plants died."

"Poor plants," Elizabeth said.

"Poor Mr. Kiebel," Dad said. "He lost a lot of money."

"Didn't he have insurance?" Mom asked.

"Yes, but—" Dad started.

"Wait!" I was very interested in Mr. Kiebel and his tomatoes. I didn't want to miss anything. "What's insurance?"

Dad frowned thoughtfully. "It's not easy to explain, but I'll try. Mr. Kiebel grows tomatoes and sells them to stores. That's how he earns money for his family."

Elizabeth and I nodded. I understood *that*!

"Most years everything goes fine," Dad went on. "The tomatoes are healthy, Mr. Kiebel sells them, and his family gets the money they need. But Mr. Kiebel is a smart and careful man.

He knows farming is a tricky business. Sooner or later something will go wrong."

"Like the flood," Elizabeth said.

Dad nodded. "That's right. But even in the years when something goes wrong, Mr. Kiebel's family still needs money. So each year he pays a small amount of money to an insurance company. In return, that company promises to give Mr. Kiebel money if something bad happens."

"Like the flood," I said.

"Right," Daddy said.

"So what happened with Mr. Kiebel?" Mom asked.

"The insurance company told him they weren't going to pay," Dad said.

"That's not fair!" Elizabeth exclaimed.

"Mr. Kiebel didn't think so either,"

Dad said. "He thought what they were doing was against the law. That's why he asked me for help."

"Did you help him?" Elizabeth asked.

"I sure did!" Dad told us. "He received his money today."

"Good for you!" Mom said.

"You're a hero!" Elizabeth said.

"Well, I don't know about that," Dad said. "And the Kiebels still have a lot of problems to deal with. Their farm is a mess from all the flooding. That's why I invited them to spend Thanksgiving with us."

"What a nice idea," Mom said, smiling. "Thanksgiving is always more fun with guests."

"Do the Kiebels have any kids?" Elizabeth asked.

"Yes," Dad told her. "They have a daughter in third grade."

I was all warmed up by now. "Come on," I said to Elizabeth. "Let's have a tea party on the bottom of the pool."

"OK," Elizabeth said.

"Wait a second," Dad said. "You haven't heard the best part yet."

"What?" I asked.

"Mr. Kiebel wants to provide the turkey for our Thanksgiving dinner," Dad announced. "He's sending a turkey from his farm. It will be delivered tomorrow."

"Really?" I asked.

"Really," Dad said.

"Yippee!" I yelled.

We were going to have turkey for Thanksgiving!

I celebrated by doing a cannonball into the pool.

Thanks to Mr. Kiebel, Thanksgiving was going to be perfect!

CHAPTER 3

A Gobbling Surprise

"What's going on?" Elizabeth asked on Friday afternoon. We had skipped all the way from the bus stop. I love Fridays! A truck was parked in front of our house. A man in dirty overalls was talking to Mom.

"I don't know," I replied. "But let's find out."

Elizabeth and I started to run. Steven was right behind us.

"You can't leave it here," Mom was telling the man as we ran up.

"I can't *not* leave it," the man said.

"Your name is right here on my delivery form. You're Mrs. Wakefield, right?"

"Right!" I yelled.

Mom frowned at me.

"What's going on?" Steven asked.

The man looked at his form again. "This is Sweet Valley, isn't it?" he asked.

"Yes!" I yelled.

"Jessica," Mom said. "Please be quiet."

"Then everything is in order," said the man. He walked around to the back of the truck, opened its big doors, and pulled out a ramp.

"What's going on?" Steven asked again.

Mom didn't answer.

But the delivery man did. "Your Thanksgiving dinner has arrived," he announced.

16

He put a huge crate on the sidewalk. "Please sign here," he told Mom.

Steven, Elizabeth, and I crouched down next to the crate.

"I think it's the biggest turkey in history," Elizabeth said.

"Me, too," I said. "And I think it's alive."

"Mom, we're opening the crate, OK?" Steven yelled.

"No!" Mom said quickly. "Not out here."

The delivery man took the form from Mom and started pulling up his ramp.

"Please," Mom said. "Please don't leave the turkey. This is a residential area. We can't have livestock here!"

"Sorry, those are my orders." He slammed the truck's doors closed and started toward the driver's seat.

"Wait," Mom said as the driver

climbed into the truck. "What do turkeys eat?"

Elizabeth and I traded looks. There really *was* a live turkey in that crate. How cool!

"He'd probably like some birdseed," the driver said. "He'll eat grass, dandelions, maybe some insects if he can find them."

Then he started up the truck. "Happy Thanksgiving!" he called as he drove away. Mom looked very upset. She just stood there watching the truck disappear.

"Let's take the crate inside!" I said.

"No!" Mom yelled. "We'll take it into the backyard."

"I'll carry it!" Steven tried to pick up the crate, but he couldn't. "It's too heavy," he complained.

So Mom carried the crate into the

backyard. Elizabeth and I made sure the gate was closed after her.

"Open it, open it," I begged, dancing around the crate.

"You kids go ahead." Mom sounded tired. "But be careful!"

Steven lifted the lid off the crate, and one of the sides fell down. There stood a surprised-looking bird. He stared curiously at each of us. Then he started to explore the backyard.

We all turned to watch him.

The bird's feathers were different shades of red and black and brown. He had a tail shaped like a fan. He was about the same height as me, but his head was much smaller.

Steven's mouth dropped open. "*That's* a turkey?"

"He's huge," Elizabeth said.

"He's beautiful," Mom said.

But something was bothering me. "Mommy?" I asked. "We aren't going to eat him, are we?"

"*I'm* not," Mom said immediately.

"Me, neither," I said.

"Me, neither," Elizabeth said.

The turkey walked up to Steven and stared him right in the face. "Me, neither," Steven added quickly.

Steven, Elizabeth, and I stayed in the backyard with the turkey all afternoon. We wanted to make sure he didn't run away or get hurt. Mostly he just poked around. He seemed to like his new home.

When Dad got home, Mom brought him out to see the turkey.

"Well, this is a surprise!" Dad said. "Mr. Kiebel didn't mention that the turkey was going to be alive! He's a beauty, isn't he?"

"What are we going to do with him?" Mom asked.

"Have him for Thanksgiving dinner," Dad said.

I could hardly believe my ears. "Daddy!" I yelled. "No!"

"We can't!" Elizabeth cried.

Steven made a face. "Really, Dad, that's gross."

Dad frowned. "I don't think we have much choice," he said. "The turkey was a gift. Mr. Kiebel would be insulted if we didn't accept it."

We all stared at Dad. He looked so serious that I was afraid to argue. Nobody else said anything, either. We all turned to watch the turkey peck at the grass. He was the best-looking bird I'd ever seen.

"Maybe we could buy a turkey at the grocery store," Steven suggested finally. "Then when the Kiebels come over, we could pretend it was this one."

That sounded like a great idea to me.

But Dad shook his head. "That would be dishonest," he said.

Mom sighed.

"I understand if you don't want to—er, cook the turkey," Dad told Mom. "Don't worry. I'll do it."

"No," Mom said quickly. "I'll do it."

Well, one thing was for sure. *I* wasn't going to do it.

CHAPTER 4

The Strangest Pet in Sweet Valley

After breakfast on Saturday morning, Lila and Amy came over to play with me and Elizabeth.

"We got a new pet!" Elizabeth announced as soon as our friends arrived.

I frowned at Elizabeth. The turkey wasn't exactly a *pet*. After all, we were supposed to eat him. But I understood why Elizabeth was excited.

We hadn't had a pet since the time we'd hidden a cat in the house. Mom and Dad had found out about Misty because she'd made Dad sneeze. We'd had to give her away. We don't have a dog because I'm afraid of them. Once in a while, we get to watch the class hamsters over the weekend. Their names are Tinkerbell and Thumbelina. I like them. Elizabeth loves them. But they're not really *ours*.

"What kind of pet?" Amy asked.

"Guess," Elizabeth said.

"A cat?" Amy asked.

"Nope, it's heavier than a cat," I said.

"A dog?" Lila guessed.

Elizabeth shook her head. "Taller than a dog."

Amy's eyes widened. "A horse?"

I rolled my eyes. Amy *would* guess a horse. She's horse crazy.

"A horse would be neat," Elizabeth said. "But that's not it. I'll give you a clue: Our new pet doesn't have any fur."

Amy got a funny look on her face. I giggled. I could tell she was trying to imagine a heavy, tall, fur-less animal.

"I'm tired of guessing," Lila said impatiently. "What is it?"

"A bird!" I announced.

"A bird that's taller than a dog?" Lila asked.

I nodded.

"I don't believe you," Lila said.

"Come see!" Elizabeth said. We headed out to the backyard. The turkey was slowly walking along the fence.

"Ooo, a peacock," Lila breathed.

Elizabeth and I laughed.

"It's a turkey!" I told Lila.

"I know," Lila said quickly. "I was just kidding."

Lila is such a big liar sometimes!

She never admits it when she makes a mistake.

"What's its name?" Amy asked.

"It doesn't have one," I said.

"Well, let's name it," Amy suggested.

"How about Penelope?" I said. "That's a name fit for a princess."

Elizabeth shook her head. "But the turkey is a *boy*."

"How do you know?" Amy asked.

"Because it *looks* like a boy," she said. I could see her point—the turkey's feathers were black and brown and bronze. Boy colors.

"It's definitely a boy," Lila agreed.

I thought for a minute. "Then how about Charles? Princes are always named Charles."

"He's not a prince," Elizabeth pointed out. "He's just a turkey."

"What do *you* think we should name him?" Amy asked.

"Tom," Elizabeth said.

"Perfect," I agreed.

"Does he bite?" Lila asked.

"No," I said.

"I don't think he has any teeth," Elizabeth added with a giggle.

"Let's play with him," Lila suggested.

"Play what?" I asked.

"Dress-up," Lila said. That's Lila's favorite game. Usually, Elizabeth and Amy can't stand it.

"OK," Elizabeth said.

Amy nodded.

I guess they thought dressing up a turkey sounded like more fun than dressing up us.

We all ran upstairs. Elizabeth found a doll hat that was just the right size for Tom. I got out a cape from last Halloween. Amy found a big bow for Tom's tail. Lila got a scarf to put around his neck.

We ran back downstairs.

Amy and Elizabeth held Tom while Lila and I dressed him. He didn't fuss at all.

He looked very, very funny when we finished.

"He's great!" Elizabeth exclaimed.

"I wish everyone could see him," Lila said.

"Let's take him for a walk!" Amy suggested.

"How?" Elizabeth asked.

"We could use a dog leash," Amy said.

"But Tom doesn't have a collar," Elizabeth pointed out. "We can't use a leash without one of those."

"Even if we had a collar, it would

be too big for his neck," I added.

Amy thought for a second. "We need a halter collar. You know, the kind people use with really big dogs."

"Ellen has one like that for Dixon!" Lila exclaimed.

Dixon is Ellen's dog. He's big and strong, so he wears a halter when Ellen walks him. With the halter, Ellen can hold him back—a little.

"Let's call her," Amy said.

Lila and I ran inside to call Ellen. She rode her bike over right away. She had Dixon's halter collar and leash with her.

Ellen was amazed to see a turkey—especially a turkey wearing clothes. "I wish I could have been here for the dress-up part!" she said.

Elizabeth and Amy put Dixon's stuff on Tom.

I tried pulling on the leash very gently. Tom stepped toward me. Slowly, I led Tom around the side of the house. Elizabeth, Amy, Lila, and Ellen followed. We all walked down the sidewalk together. Caroline Pearce saw us from her window. She came outside and walked with us. It was like a parade!

We took turns holding the leash. We walked Tom all the way to the park. It took a long time to get there because Tom kept stopping to peck at the ground. People driving by slowed down and waved to us.

Lots of our friends were at the park when we got there. Everyone ran over to meet Tom.

"He has such pretty feathers," Eva Simpson said.

"And such sensitive eyes!" Lois Waller said.

"Are you going to keep him forever?" Todd Wilkins asked.

Elizabeth and I traded sad looks. We hadn't told any of our friends *why* we had Tom. But now we had to.

"Dad wants to eat him for Thanksgiving dinner." I whispered, so that Tom couldn't hear.

Eva's eyes got big.

Lois looked like she was going to cry.

Caroline made a face.

"We've got to save him!" Todd sounded determined.

"How?" Elizabeth asked.

"We'll think of a plan together," Amy said.

I held Tom's leash while everyone thought and thought. Tom pecked at the ground, looking for insects. I don't think he knew what we were thinking about.

After a long time, Lila came up with a perfect plan. Then everyone said good-bye to Tom. Elizabeth and I smiled all the way home.

We knew what we had to do to save Tom's life.

CHAPTER 5

Plan A

"Are you ready?" Elizabeth asked me on Monday afternoon. We were in our room. We had just got home from school, and it was time to put our plan into action.

"I think so," I replied. "But I'm a little nervous."

"Don't worry," Elizabeth said. "You're a terrific actress. You'll be great!"

That made me feel better.

"Thanks," I said. "Let's go!"

We got up and tiptoed downstairs.

I went into the bathroom and closed the door.

"Mommy!" I heard Elizabeth yell from the hallway. "Mommy, come quick!"

"What's the matter?" called Mom.

"Jessica's sick," Elizabeth said. "I think she just threw up."

Footsteps hurried up to the bathroom door.

My heart was beating double time. Could I really pull this off?

"Honey, are you OK?" Mom called to me. "Let me in."

Taking a deep breath, I opened the bathroom door. I hugged my stomach as I walked out. "I don't feel good," I groaned.

"You look terrible," Elizabeth said, playing along.

"Did you throw up?" Mom asked.

I nodded.

Mom put her hand on my forehead. "You don't feel hot, but I want to take your temperature. Come into the kitchen—I left something on the stove."

Mom got a thermometer out of the medicine cabinet, and then Elizabeth and I followed her into the kitchen. Mom popped the thermometer into my mouth as soon as I sat down. When she turned to the stove, I pulled out the thermometer and looked at it. Maybe I could *make* myself have a fever! But I didn't know how to read it, so I just stuck it back into my mouth. Just in time, too! Mom turned back from the stove. "Have you been feeling sick all day?" she asked.

That was the question I had been waiting for.

I shook my head as hard as I could.

Then I tried to talk around the thermometer. "Jrust since lrurnch."

"Just since lunch," Elizabeth repeated. "I think she's sick because of something she ate."

"That's strange," Mom said. "I packed the same things I always pack."

"That's what *I* ate," Elizabeth said. "But Jessica forgot her lunch on the bus."

Mom turned worried eyes on me. I did my best to look awful. "What did Jessica have for lunch?" she asked.

"She shared with Lila," Elizabeth said. "Potato chips and a turkey sandwich."

I was impressed with Elizabeth's performance. She doesn't like to lie. But she was actually pretty good at it.

Mom took the thermometer out of my mouth. She read the numbers. "Normal," she announced. Elizabeth and I traded worried looks. Mom was staring at me thoughtfully. "A *turkey* sandwich, huh?"

I nodded. Then I gave a loud groan, just for effect.

"I was thinking," Elizabeth said. "Maybe turkey makes Jessica sick. You know, the way cats make Dad and Steven sick."

"You mean Jessica is allergic to turkey?" Mom asked.

"Yup!" Elizabeth said.

A smile slowly spread over Mom's face. "I think you must be right."

"You do?" I exclaimed. Elizabeth frowned at me. "Oh—of course you do," I added quickly.

"I guess we'd better not have turkey for Thanksgiving dinner," Elizabeth said.

"I guess not," Mom agreed.

"Hurray!" I was so happy, I started to dance around the kitchen.

Elizabeth joined in.

Mom laughed.

Right in the middle of our dance, the back door opened and Dad came in.

Elizabeth stopped dancing.

I was too happy to stop.

"What's going on?" Dad sounded surprised.

"We're having a party!" I said.

"Why?" Dad asked.

"Because we can't have Tom for Thanksgiving," I said.

"Why not?" Dad asked.

"Because I ate a turkey sandwich for lunch and it made me sick," I said.

Elizabeth was shaking her head and waving her hands in front of her face. She's weird sometimes.

Then I realized what she meant.

Sick people don't dance. I grabbed my stomach and groaned.

But it was too late.

"You don't look sick," Dad said.

"Mom took her temperature," Elizabeth said.

Dad looked at Mom. "It was normal," Mom admitted.

"I feel really awful," I insisted.

"Maybe," Dad said. "But even if you do feel sick, it could be for any number of reasons. The turkey sandwich wasn't necessarily causing the trouble."

"Does this mean we have to have Tom for Thanksgiving?" Elizabeth asked.

Dad nodded. "I've told you girls before, I can't insult Mr. Kiebel by refusing his gift. That turkey is so big, he must be worth a lot of money. It was a generous present, and we're going to accept it. If Jessica has a sudden allergy to turkey, she can stick with mashed potatoes and stuffing."

Elizabeth looked very sad. So did Mom.

I was starting to feel awful for real. It was all my fault Dad had figured out the truth. If I hadn't been dancing around, Tom's life might have been saved.

"Let's go say hello to Tom," Elizabeth suggested quietly.

"OK," I agreed.

When Elizabeth and I stepped outside, Tom ran right up to us.

I rested my head against his feathery side. "Don't worry, Tom," I whispered to him. "We're not going to give up. We'll think of another way to save you."

I didn't tell Tom that time was running out. Thanksgiving was only three days away.

CHAPTER 6

A Close Call

That evening, Dad was watching his favorite TV show—a news show called *Wall Street*. *Wall Street* isn't much like *Sesame Street*. *Wall Street* is bor-ing!

Elizabeth and I were playing a board game, but neither of us was really interested in it. We could see Tom through the window. He was walking around outside, pecking the ground. I thought he looked lonely. Maybe he missed his family.

The phone rang.

"Would one of you girls get that?" Dad didn't take his eyes from the screen.

"Sure!" I jumped up and skipped into the kitchen. I didn't mind leaving the game. Elizabeth was winning, anyway.

I picked up the phone. "Hello?"

"Hello," came a voice. "Is Ned Wakefield at home?"

Ned Wakefield is my dad. But I didn't call him right away. Dad hates to be interrupted during *Wall Street*. Besides, I didn't recognize the voice on the other end of the line.

"May I tell him who's calling?" I asked in my best polite voice.

"Mr. Kiebel," answered the man.

Mr. Kiebel was the farmer who had sent us Tom! I wondered what he wanted.

"Just a minute, please," I said.

Carefully, I put the phone down. I ran into the den.

"Dad, Mr. Kiebel is on the phone," I announced.

Dad immediately switched off the TV. He walked into the kitchen.

Elizabeth jumped up, too. "Come on!" she told me. "Let's find out what Mr. Kiebel wants. Maybe he's sick and he can't come to Thanksgiving dinner."

We ran into the kitchen together.

Dad was just picking up the phone. "Mr. Kiebel?" he said. "How are you?"

There was a pause while Dad listened.

"Yes, it got here just fine," Dad said. "Came on Friday."

"Mr. Kiebel must be asking about

46

Tom," I whispered to Elizabeth.

She nodded.

"No, we like him just fine," Dad said into the phone.

"Mr. Kiebel must be worried we don't like Tom," I whispered to Elizabeth.

She nodded impatiently. "I know!"

Dad put his fingers to his lips.

Geez! Nobody appreciates me.

"You want to take him back?" Dad asked. He sounded surprised.

Elizabeth and I traded looks. This was great news! Of course, we would be sorry to lose our pet. But that would be better than eating him.

I crossed my fingers and hoped Dad would agree.

"There's no need for you to take him back," Dad said.

I groaned.

"I promise you," Dad said, "we love the turkey."

And we *did* love Tom. That was the problem.

A minute later Dad hung up.

"What did Mr. Kiebel want?" I asked.

"Why did you tell him we wouldn't give Tom back to him?" Elizabeth asked. "If we sent him back, we wouldn't have to eat him."

Dad looked sad. "I know it's hard to understand, girls," he said. "But it's important for me to be on good terms with Mr. Kiebel, because he's my client. And it would be rude to send back his gift. Do you understand that?"

We nodded. "But I don't want to eat Tom, Daddy," I said. "He's a nice turkey. Why does Mr. Kiebel want to have him for dinner?"

"I don't want to eat him, either, sweetheart," Daddy said. "But this might be a good lesson for you girls. You always loved turkey before, Jess. Well, Mr. Kiebel is a farmer, and turkeys come from farms. Eating Tom is no different from eating a turkey we buy in a store. Mr. Kiebel isn't being mean. He just lives a different lifestyle. For him, it's not strange to raise a turkey only to eat it."

"I know turkeys from the store are just the same," Elizabeth said. "But it seems different now that we've met Tom."

"I'm sorry you've got so attached to the turkey," Dad said. Then he went back into the den to catch the rest of his show.

Elizabeth and I stayed in the kitchen.

"If only Dad had told Mr. Kiebel that we don't want to eat a turkey we know," Elizabeth said. "It might have saved Tom's life."

"Well, he didn't," I said. "So it's up to us to save Tom's life."

"But we *tried* already!" Elizabeth wailed.

"If at first you don't succeed, try, try again," I said. Mrs. Otis is always telling us that.

Elizabeth nodded. "Plan A failed. What we need now is Plan B."

CHAPTER 7

Plan B

"Hey, you guys!" Steven called the next day after school. "Sit over here!"

Elizabeth and I had just climbed onto the bus.

"I saved you a seat!" Steven added.

Elizabeth and I looked at each other in surprise. Steven had never, ever saved us seats on the bus before. In fact, he usually ignored us when other kids were around. He liked to pretend we weren't related. When he *did* admit to knowing us, it was only so he could tease us.

"Us?" Elizabeth asked Steven.

"Yes," Steven said with an impatient frown. "Hurry up and sit down. It's important."

Elizabeth gave a little shrug. We slid into the seat Steven had saved. It was right in front of his.

"What do you want?" I asked.

"I know how we can save Tom," Steven announced.

"Really?" I asked. "How?"

The bus lurched forward.

"My teacher told us that every year at Thanksgiving the President rescues a turkey," Steven said. "It's called a turkey pardon. So I was thinking, maybe Tom can be the turkey this year!"

"The president of what?" I asked.

Steven rolled his eyes. "The President of the United States of America. *The* President."

"But we don't know the President," I reminded Steven.

"No duh!" he said.

I don't like it when my brother acts like I'm stupid. "If we don't know him, how can we ask him a favor?" I demanded.

"I don't know!" Steven yelled. "I haven't worked out every little part of this plan."

"Why don't we write him a letter?" Elizabeth asked.

Steven and I both stared at her.

"A *very* good idea," Steven said. He stuck his tongue out at me. "See? I told you it was no big problem."

Ha! Steven never would have figured that out on his own.

"We can write the letter in my room," Steven said when we got home.

Steven rarely lets us into his room.

He even has a sign on the door that reads NO GIRLS ALLOWED. There could be only one reason why Steven was inviting us in. He wanted to save Tom just as much as we did.

Steven dumped some comic books from his desk onto the floor. He pushed some dirty clothes off his desk chair and sat down. "I'll write," he said importantly.

"How come?" I demanded.

"Because I'm older and I know cursive," Steven said. "We can't print a letter to the President."

"We know how to write cursive, too," I said. "We learned this year."

"Yeah, but we want the President to be able to *read* our letter," Steven said. "And everyone knows baby's handwriting is hard to read."

Didn't I tell you Steven was a pain?

"You can write the letter," Elizabeth told Steven.

"But we get to help decide what to say," I added.

"Fine," Steven said.

Writing the letter took a super-long time. We argued over just about every word. When it was finally finished, this is what it said:

Dear President of the United States of America,

Hi! How are you?

We are not so good. We are sad about our friend Tom. He is a turkey. Our dad wants to eat him for Thanksgiving dinner.

Please help us save Tom! He is really very nice. You could give him a turkey pardon.

Thank you so much!

"I think I should sign my name first," Steven said when the letter was finished.

"No way!" I wanted to sign my name first so the President would see it first.

"Yes way," Steven said. "The letter was my idea."

"Was not!" I said. "It was Elizabeth's idea."

Steven's face was red. "Well, I should sign first because I'm the oldest."

"That's dumb," I argued. "*I* should sign first because I'm Tom's favorite."

Elizabeth sighed. "We can sign it in a row across the bottom," she suggested.

"I want my name on the left side," Steven said immediately.

"Just sign it!" Elizabeth yelled.

Geez! She is so touchy sometimes.

Steven picked up the pencil and wrote his name.

I smiled at Elizabeth. "Some people will argue about *anything*."

"Yeah," Elizabeth said. "Some people—like you!"

That wasn't fair! I would have argued with her, but it seemed as if Elizabeth was in a bad mood. She took the pencil from Steven, wrote her name on the letter, and shoved the pencil at me. While I was writing, Elizabeth found an envelope. She folded up the letter and put it inside.

"Oh, no," Elizabeth said.

"What's wrong?" I asked.

"We don't have the President's address," Elizabeth said.

"No problem," Steven told her. "We can get it at the post office. I'm sure they know it. Lots of people must write to the President."

"Not too many, I hope," Elizabeth said. "If he gets lots and lots of letters, he might not see ours right away."

"He will," I said. "He has to."

"Let's go mail it right away," Elizabeth said. "The sooner it gets to the White House, the better."

"OK!" I agreed.

Steven, Elizabeth, and I asked permission to go to the post office. Mom said it was OK to ride our bikes there.

At the post office, we had to wait in a long line. When we finally got to the front, we gave our letter to the clerk.

"There's no address on this," the clerk said.

"We want to send it to the President," I told her.

"Do you know his address?" Elizabeth asked.

The clerk smiled. "Not by heart. But I bet I can find it for you."

"I told you so," Steven said, sticking his tongue out at me and Elizabeth.

We didn't pay any attention to him.

The clerk got out a big book. She flipped through the pages until she found the President's address: 1600 Pennsylvania Avenue in Washington, D.C. Elizabeth wrote it on the envelope.

"You're all set!" the clerk said, taking the letter. "By the way, why are you writing the President?"

Elizabeth explained about Tom.

The clerk started to frown.

"What's wrong?" I asked.

"Thanksgiving is the day after tomorrow," the clerk reminded us.

"So?" I asked.

"Your letter won't get to Washington until after the holiday," the clerk said.

"But that will be too late to save Tom," Elizabeth said.

The clerk nodded. "I'm sorry."

"Come on," Elizabeth said sadly. "Let's go."

I was very worried as I followed Steven and Elizabeth out of the post office. We had to find a way to save Tom.

Time was running out.

CHAPTER 8

Plans C Through Z

"Maybe Tom could run away and join the circus," Lila suggested on Wednesday.

Elizabeth and I were eating lunch with our friends. We were all trying to think of another way to save Tom. "I don't think Tom would be good in the circus," I said. "He doesn't know any tricks."

"Maybe you could teach him," Ellen said hopefully.

"I don't think so," Elizabeth said.

"He's not that smart," I explained.

Elizabeth and I had spent a lot of time watching Tom. We had decided he wasn't very bright. The evening before, I had been sitting on the lawn. Elizabeth had put some new seed out for Tom. In his hurry to get to it, Tom had run right over me!

"If he's not smart," Andy said, "maybe you can convince him he's a robin."

"What good would that do?" I asked.

"You could get him to migrate!" Andy started to laugh, and then to cough. His eyes bugged out.

Lila rolled her eyes. Andy has a weird sense of humor.

"Maybe you could give Tom to a zoo," Todd suggested.

"That's a good idea!" I said.

But Elizabeth shook her head.

"When was the last time you saw a turkey in the zoo?"

I groaned. "I wish the Kiebels weren't coming to Thanksgiving at our house. Then they wouldn't know what we did with Tom."

"That would be great," Elizabeth agreed.

"Why don't you call and *un*invite them?" Amy suggested.

"We can't do that," Elizabeth said.

"Mom and Dad would get mad," I said. "And if we did that, the Kiebels wouldn't have anywhere to go for Thanksgiving."

"Maybe someone else will invite them over," Ellen said hopefully. "Someone they like better."

Elizabeth's face brightened. "Maybe we can make sure someone else invites them." Then Elizabeth told us

64

what she had in mind: Maybe we could get *ourselves* invited somewhere else for Thanksgiving. After all, if we weren't at our house, we couldn't have the Kiebels over.

I wasn't sure it would work. But it was our only chance.

When we got home that afternoon, Mom was sitting in the backyard. She was reading a book.

"Look," Mom said softly as Elizabeth and I came out of the house.

We tiptoed forward. Tom was lying by Mom's side. He was snuggled up next to her just like a cat!

Mom was smiling. "He wandered over to me just after I sat down."

Elizabeth and I knelt next to Tom. We took turns petting him. His feathers fluffed up. He made a happy gurgling

sound and chirped at us. Tom liked to be petted. He liked *us*. And he *trusted* us. We had to do something to protect him.

"Mom, can we call Aunt Helen?" I asked.

Aunt Helen is actually Mom's aunt. She's our great-aunt. She is also one of our absolutely favorite relatives. She lives about an hour away. We're not allowed to call her without permission because it's long-distance.

My question surprised Mom. "Why do you want to call Aunt Helen?" she asked.

Elizabeth and I traded looks. We couldn't tell Mom the *real* reason.

I thought fast. "We—um, want to wish her a happy Thanksgiving."

"I'm sure she'd love that," Mom

said. "Do you want me to come in and dial for you?"

"No," I said quickly. "We don't want to disturb Tom."

"We can do it," Elizabeth added.

"OK," Mom said. "Come and get me if you have any problems."

Elizabeth and I hurried into the house. We wanted to make our call before Mom came inside, or Dad got home.

I looked up Aunt Helen's number in Mom's phone book.

Elizabeth dialed.

"Hello?" came a voice.

"Aunt Helen? It's Jessica!"

"Why, hello, sweetie! How are you?"

"Not so good," I said. "I have a big problem."

"Maybe I can help," Aunt Helen said.

"I hope so," I said. Then I told her all about Tom. "So could you please invite our family over for Thanksgiving?" I asked when I finished. "It's the only way we can think of to save Tom."

"I'm so sorry," Aunt Helen said. "I feel terrible about Tom. But I can't help. I'm leaving for the airport in an hour."

"Where are you going?"

"New York City," Aunt Helen said. "I'm meeting a friend. We're going to see the Thanksgiving parade."

"Oh. Well, have fun," I said.

"I'll try," Aunt Helen said. "And you try not to worry too much about Tom. I know you kids will think of something. You're good at getting out of scrapes."

After I hung up the phone, I told

Elizabeth what Aunt Helen had said.

Elizabeth looked very sad. I *felt* very sad. It was nice that Aunt Helen had confidence in us. But she had been our last chance. We'd never save Tom now.

CHAPTER 9

Sleepless Night

That night, I tossed and turned. I turned and tossed. I could not sleep. All I could think about was Tom. Thanksgiving was the next day, and we hadn't found a way to save him.

About an hour after we had gone to bed, Elizabeth sat up. "I can't sleep," she announced. "Let's go downstairs and say good-bye to Tom."

"OK," I agreed right away.

Elizabeth led the way out of our room. We tiptoed down the stairs and toward the door to the backyard. That's in the kitchen.

It was the middle of the night. But guess what?

Mom was sitting at the kitchen table!

"What are you girls doing out of bed?" she asked.

"We wanted to say good-bye to Tom," Elizabeth explained.

"Me, too," said a voice behind us.

Elizabeth and I spun around. Steven was standing in the hallway. He was dressed in his pajamas. He looked very unhappy.

"Well, don't say good-bye yet," Mom said.

"Why not?" Elizabeth asked.

"I just can't stand the idea of anyone hurting Tom," Mom said. "I have a plan to save him."

"Hurray!" I yelled.

"Yippee!" Elizabeth yelled.

"Cool!" Steven exclaimed.

"Shh," Mom said. "We don't want to wake up your father. You know he'd feel guilty about not using the Kiebels' gift."

"Tell us about your plan," Elizabeth whispered.

"Well, the first part is finding a place to hide Tom," Mom said.

We talked about it and decided the toolshed would be the best place.

Like quiet little mice, Elizabeth and I pulled the tools out of the shed. Steven and Mom carried them into the basement. Elizabeth put some leaves from the compost heap down on the toolshed floor. I poured some seed into a bowl.

Tom was curious about what we

73

were doing. He came over to find out why we were in the shed. As soon as he was inside, Elizabeth and I sneaked out. We closed the door behind us. Tom was locked in.

"Do you think he'll be OK?" Elizabeth sounded worried. "It's awfully dark in there."

"Only because it's dark outside," Mom said. "Once the sun comes up, light will come through the windows."

"What if someone hears him gobble?" Steven asked.

Mom thought for a second. "We'll just have to keep everyone out of the backyard," she said.

"What are you going to tell Dad?" I asked.

"You'll find out in the morning," Mom said. "But now it's time for bed—tomorrow's a big day. Don't worry about Tom."

"Are you sure your plan will work?" Elizabeth asked.

"Positive," Mom said. I liked having Mom on our side!

CHAPTER 10

Fooling Dad

"Jessica, wake up!"

I opened my eyes. Elizabeth was bouncing on her bed. Sunlight streamed into our window.

"Happy Thanksgiving!" Elizabeth said.

"Happy Thanksgiving!" I said. "Let's go find out what's happening with Tom."

Elizabeth and I jumped out of our beds. We got dressed quickly. Then we ran downstairs.

Mom and Steven were already in

the kitchen. Steven was stirring something in a huge bowl. The turkey pan was on the kitchen counter.

"What's going on?" I asked. "Where's Dad?"

Mom winked at me. "He's still sleeping, and we're cooking a turkey."

Elizabeth looked worried. "Tom?"

Mom shook her head. "Tom is safe in his new home. I took him some fresh seed earlier."

Steven pointed to the bowl in front of him. "Our turkey is in there."

I peeked into the bowl. "But it's just some dough."

"Sticky dough," Steven added. "I've been stirring it for ten whole minutes. My arm is about to fall off!"

"You can stop now," Mom told Steven. Then she turned to Elizabeth and me. "We're going to

78

make a turkey out of dough," she whispered.

"Like in art class?" Elizabeth asked.

"Right," Mom said.

I frowned. This did not sound like a good plan.

"But, Mom," I said, "when you cut the turkey, everyone will know it's a fake."

Mom smiled. "Then we won't cut it."

"I don't understand," I complained.

"Trust me," Mom said. "But right now we have to hurry. No more questions."

Elizabeth, Steven, and I got to work. We shaped the dough around a metal coffee can. Mom helped. About twenty minutes later, we had a fake turkey that was almost the same shape as the real thing.

Mom put the dough turkey in the turkey pan. She covered it with melted butter. Then she slipped it into the oven.

"When your dad comes down, I'll do the talking," Mom said.

"That's good," Elizabeth said.

"It sure is," I agreed. "I have no idea what's going to happen."

"You'll find out soon," Mom said mysteriously.

Mom made us scrambled eggs and cinnamon toast for breakfast. While we were eating, I smelled something funny.

"Mom, the turkey is burning!" I cried.

"I know," Mom said. "Everything is going according to plan."

It *was*? How interesting. I was curious to see what would happen next. I could hardly wait for Dad to come downstairs.

We finished eating. We did the breakfast dishes. Mom made an apple pie. All that time our dough turkey stayed in the oven. Mom didn't turn it off until it was burned to a crisp.

Finally, after what seemed like forever, we heard Dad's footsteps on the stairs. "Is something burning?" he asked as he came into the kitchen.

Mom put on a sad face. "Yes, the lovely turkey Mr. Kiebel sent us. I'm afraid we'll have to throw it out. It's too burned to eat."

I held my breath while Dad peeked into the oven. Would the dough turkey fool him?

Dad turned back to us. He looked surprised. "Alice," he said to Mom, "did

you get Tom—I mean, the turkey— ready to cook all by yourself?"

Mom didn't answer right away. The question must have surprised her. I crossed my fingers and hoped Dad wouldn't discover the truth.

Elizabeth had her fingers crossed, too.

Say something quick! I tried to beam the message into Mom's head.

"Actually, I had a little help," Mom said. "From the butcher shop."

Dad made a face. He didn't ask any more questions. He just poured himself a cup of coffee and sat down at the table. I still wasn't sure whether we had fooled him.

"Are you upset?" I asked Dad.

"No," he said. "I'm glad the turkey burned."

"How come?" Elizabeth asked.

Dad smiled. "I didn't want to eat Tom any more than you kids did."

"Then why did you say we had to?" Elizabeth asked.

"Like I told you, I didn't want to hurt Mr. Kiebel's feelings," Dad said. "I just hope he won't be too disappointed now."

Elizabeth looked worried.

Mom looked a little bit guilty.

I knew they were all hoping Mr. Kiebel would understand. *I* just hoped he wouldn't ask too many questions. Or go into the backyard and hear Tom gobble.

Lots of things could go wrong during dinner.

It was going to be a very long Thanksgiving.

CHAPTER 11

Grumpy Guests

By two o'clock, my whole family was dressed in their holiday clothes. Elizabeth and I were wearing beautiful party dresses.

The doorbell rang.

We all went to greet the Kiebels.

"Happy Thanksgiving!" Mom said as she opened the door.

"Welcome!" Dad added.

"Hello," the Kiebels all said quietly. None of them looked very happy.

Mr. Kiebel was wearing a blue shirt and a baseball cap with letters on it.

He had very strong-looking arms.

Mrs. Kiebel was carrying an apple pie. She had on a pretty yellow sundress.

The Kiebels' daughter had two long bright-red braids and big freckles all over her face.

Everyone came inside.

"This is Clara," Mrs. Kiebel said to Elizabeth, Steven, and me.

We all told Clara our names.

"I'm glad you're here," Elizabeth added.

"We're going to have fun," I put in. "We have lots of toys. You can play with whatever you like."

"That's nice." Clara spoke so softly, I could hardly hear her. And she did not smile.

What was wrong with Clara? Why was she acting so grumpy? I hoped she cheered up soon. If she didn't, Thanksgiving wouldn't be much fun. I could tell Elizabeth was confused, too.

Steven stuck out his tongue. "Three girls," he said, making an ugly face. "Dad, can I go ride my bike, *please*?"

"Sure," Dad said. "Just change your clothes first. You don't want to get your good things dirty."

"All right!" Steven said. He hates wearing dress-up clothes.

"Make sure you come home in an hour," Mom added. "You don't want to miss dinner."

"I would never do that!" Steven said. He hurried upstairs to change.

I was jealous. Steven got to go play. Elizabeth and I were stuck with Clara the grump.

"Why don't we take that pie into

the kitchen?" Mom said to Mrs. Kiebel.

"I have some papers for you to sign," Dad told Mr. Kiebel.

The adults wandered away.

Elizabeth smiled at Clara. "Um— maybe we could go swimming before dinner," she suggested.

"No, we can't!" I said quickly.

Elizabeth frowned. "Why not?"

"You remember," I said. "We're not allowed to go into the backyard."

Elizabeth gave me a funny look. "How come?"

"The toolshed, remember?" I said.

Elizabeth gasped. "Oh. Right!"

Clara stared at us silently. Her pale-blue eyes were red, as if she had been crying.

Mom came back out into the hallway. "You haven't set the table yet," she reminded Elizabeth and me. "Why don't you do it before you start playing?"

I usually hate to set the table. But this time I was glad to do it. Even boring chores were more fun than talking to Clara.

Elizabeth and I ran into the kitchen. Clara followed us slowly.

Mrs. Kiebel was standing at the counter unwrapping her pie. "I only baked this halfway," she told Mom.

"Then why don't you pop it into the oven?" Mom suggested.

I pulled open the drawer where we keep our good silver. I love the way it sparkles. "How many people will there be at dinner?" I asked Clara and Elizabeth.

Elizabeth counted in her head. "Eight."

Clara didn't say anything.

I counted out eight forks and handed them to Elizabeth. Then I started to count out spoons to Clara.

Mrs. Kiebel opened the oven. "What's this?" she exclaimed.

"Is something wrong?" Mom asked.

"Where is the turkey?" Mrs. Kiebel was staring into the oven. Nothing was in there but two pans of Dad's famous zucchini lasagna. We had thrown out the dough turkey earlier.

"Oh, well, I'm afraid I have bad news about the turkey," Mom said uneasily.

I looked at Clara. Fat tears were standing in her eyes. What was wrong with her?

"I . . . burned it," Mom went on. "I—I had to throw it out."

Clara took a noisy, shaky breath.

She let the spoons she was holding fall to the floor. Sobbing, she ran out of the kitchen.

Mrs. Kiebel hurried after her. "Clara! Clara—come back!"

"What was that all about?" Mom wondered out loud.

"I don't know," I said. "But it sure was weird!"

"Let's go find them," Elizabeth suggested.

The three of us hurried after Clara and Mrs. Kiebel. We found them in the den with Dad and Mr. Kiebel.

Clara was hugging her father and sobbing.

Mr. Kiebel looked very upset. "Don't cry, honey," he said, patting Clara's back. "There's nothing we can do about the turkey now."

"Maybe it's best if we leave," Mrs. Kiebel said to Mr. Kiebel.

Dad had an enormous frown on his face.

I felt terrible. Somehow we had made Clara cry. Mr. and Mrs. Kiebel seemed upset, too. Maybe we'd even got Dad into trouble with them.

Thanksgiving was ruined.

CHAPTER 12

A Happy Reunion

"**I**'m very sorry about the turkey," Dad said. "We didn't mean to burn it."

"No, *I'm* sorry," Mr. Kiebel said. "I made a terrible mistake. I never should have sent it to you."

"Why not?" I asked.

"We have lots of turkeys on the farm," Mrs. Kiebel explained. "But that particular one was Clara's pet."

Elizabeth's mouth dropped open. "It *was*?"

"Poor Clara!" I exclaimed. No

wonder our guest was grumpy. And who could blame her for crying? I would have been crying, too!

"I thought that turkey seemed awfully tame," Mom said.

Dad looked really miserable now. As far as he knew, Mom really *had* burned Tom. "Why didn't you tell us?" he asked Mr. Kiebel.

"I tried," Mr. Kiebel replied. "Remember when I called—"

"But I never guessed you *really* wanted the turkey back!" Dad exclaimed. "I thought you were just worried that we didn't like it."

Everyone was so unhappy. I couldn't stand keeping our secret a second longer. I gave Mom a questioning look.

She nodded.

I reached for Clara's hand. "Come

on. I have something to show you."

Clara didn't move. She was still crying.

Elizabeth reached for Clara's other hand. "It's important," she said.

Clara let the two of us lead her into the backyard. Except for Mom, the adults looked puzzled. But they followed us, too.

This was going to be a dramatic reunion. I made sure to open the shed door with a grand gesture. Then I stepped back to show off the turkey. Tom stood majestically in the doorway of the shed. Until he saw Clara. Then he gave a loud squawk and rushed out.

"Laurabel!" Clara dashed forward and gave Tom a big hug. "Oh, Laurabel, I'm so happy you're alive!"

"Laurabel?" I repeated. "You mean Tom is a *girl*?"

Clara giggled. A beautiful smile lit up her face. "Sure, silly. What did you think?"

I gave Elizabeth a hard look. "*Some* people thought she looked like a boy."

She just shrugged.

"I'm confused," Mr. Kiebel said to Dad. "I thought you had prepared the turkey for dinner."

"That's what I thought, too," Dad said. He raised an eyebrow at Mom.

"I couldn't do it," Mom admitted. "The kids fell in love with Tom—I mean, Laurabel. So did I. I'm sorry, Mrs. Kiebel, but I'm just not used to eating animals I've seen alive."

Mrs. Kiebel chuckled.

"But what about the burned turkey I saw?" Dad asked.

"We made that out of dough to fool you," Mom said.

Dad looked very surprised and a tiny bit hurt. "I knew you didn't want to hurt Mr. Kiebel's feelings," Mom explained. "I thought you'd be happier if you didn't know about the real turkey." Then Dad looked less hurt.

"Well, I'm glad you did it!" Mr. Kiebel said.

"Me, too!" Clara exclaimed.

"Me, too," Dad said, starting to smile.

Steven ran into the backyard. "Is dinner ready yet? Hey, who let Tom out?"

"Tom?" I gave my brother a superior look. "For your information, Steven, that's a *girl* turkey."

Steven looked confused when we all laughed.

"Come on," Mom said. "Let's go inside. I don't want the lasagna to burn.

It was almost finished when we came out."

"Goody!" Clara said. "Suddenly I'm starving."

"Hey! What's going on?" Steven yelled as we headed for the house.

It was the most wonderful Thanksgiving Day ever! We all stuffed ourselves on Dad's famous zucchini lasagna. Clara was fun to talk to now that she was happy. I even talked Mom and Dad into letting Laurabel join us in the dining room.

After all, it wouldn't be Thanksgiving without a turkey!

Kaitlyn

In the puzzle below, you will find ten things people usually eat at Thanksgiving. The words are written forward, backward, and diagonally. How many can you find?

1. CIDER
2. POTATOES
3. TURKEY
4. YAMS
5. STUFFING
6. PIE
7. CRANBERRY SAUCE
8. BREAD
9. PEAS
10. GRAVY

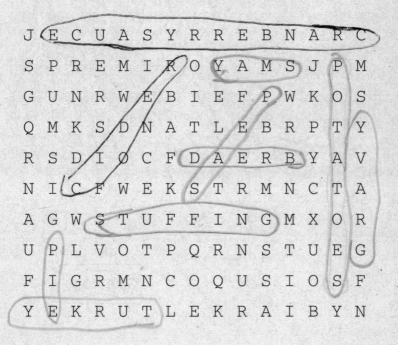

```
J E C U A S Y R R E B N A R C
S P R E M I R O Y A M S J P M
G U N R W E B I E F P W K O S
Q M K S D N A T L E B R P T Y
R S D I O C F D A E R B Y A V
N I C F W E K S T R M N C T A
A G W S T U F F I N G M X O R
U P L V O T P Q R N S T U E G
F I G R M N C O Q U S I O S F
Y E K R U T L E K R A I B Y N
```

Help the turkey find his way back to the coop!

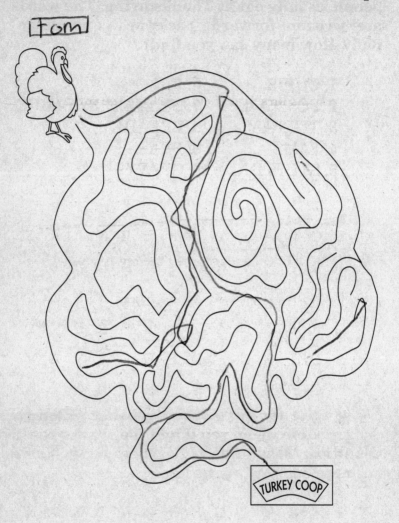

How much do you remember from Elizabeth and Jessica's Turkey Tale? Answer these trivia questions to find out:

1. What did the turkey arrive in? A c r a t e.

2. Turkeys have _ e a t _ e r s instead of fur.

3. Where did Mrs. Wakefield hide Tom the turkey?
In the t o o l s h e d.

4. The President lives at 1600 p e n n _ o _ _ _ _ _
Avenue.

5. Elizabeth and Jessica's class hamsters are named
_ _ _ o _ _ _ _ _ and Thumbelina.

6. What did Jessica pretend made her sick? A turkey
S u n d w i c h

7. When the President rescues a turkey, it's called a
turkey _ _ _ _ o _.

8. What did Amy put on Tom's tail? A _ _ o.

9. The girls put a _ _ _ _ o on Tom to walk him outside.

10. Clara told the girls the turkey was a _ o _ _!

11. Jessica's mom took her temperature with a
_ _ _ _ o _ _ _ _ _ _.

Now write the circled letters below. When you unscramble them, you'll find the answer to this question: Why didn't Elizabeth and Jessica want to eat Tom the turkey?

Because _ _ _ _ _ _ _ _ _ _ _ !

Answers

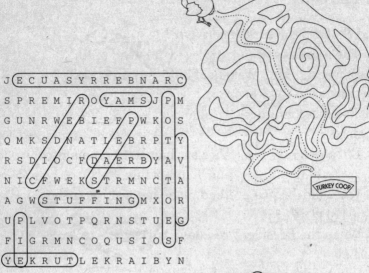

```
J E C U A S Y R R E B N A R C
S P R E M I R O Y A M S J P M
G U N R W E B I E F P W K O S
Q M K S D N A T L E B R P T Y
R S D I O C F D A E R B Y A V
N I C F W E K S T R M N C T A
A G W S T U F F I N G M X O R
U P L V O T P Q R N S T U E G
F I G R M N C O Q U S I O S F
Y E K R U T L E K R A I B Y N
```

TURKEY COOP

1. CRA**T**E
2. FEA**TH**ERS
3. TOOLSH**E**D
4. PENNS**Y**LVANIA
5. TIN**K**ERBELL
6. SA**N**DWICH
7. PARD**O**N
8. BO**W**
9. LEAS**H**
10. G**I**RL
11. THER**M**OMETER

THEY KNOW HIM

SIGN UP FOR THE
SWEET VALLEY HIGH®
FAN CLUB!

Hey, girls! Get all the gossip on Sweet
Valley High's® most popular teenagers
when you join our fantastic Fan Club!
As a member, you'll get all of this really
cool stuff:

- Membership Card with your own
  personal Fan Club ID number
- A Sweet Valley High® Secret
  Treasure Box
- Sweet Valley High® Stationery
- Official Fan Club Pencil (for secret
  note writing!)
- Three Bookmarks
- A "Members Only" Door Hanger
- Two Skeins of J. & P. Coats® Embroidery
  Floss with flower barrette instruction
  leaflet
- Two editions of *The Oracle* newsletter
- Plus exclusive Sweet Valley High®
  product offers, special savings,
  contests, and much more!

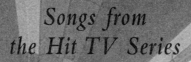

Songs from the Hit TV Series

Featuring:

"Rose Colored Glasses"

"Lotion"

"Sweet Valley High Theme"

Available on CD and Cassette Wherever Music is Sold.